SOccer Star

MICHAEL HARDCASTLE

Illustrated by Ken

🍌 YELLOW BANANAS

To Sam

K.C.

Chapter One

OSCAR COULDN'T WAIT to get home. They'd all want to hear his fantastic news. They'd all tell him he was wonderful. Well, he hoped they would. Sometimes his mum didn't seem to understand how much football meant to him. Now she would find out.

He was rushing past the play park when Jack caught sight of him.

'Hey, Oz, come and have a game,' Jack yelled. 'Simon says he'll keep goal for us.'

Oscar slowed down, torn between going home and having a kick around. The kick around won. He could also tell Jack his news.

'I'm in the team,' he burst out, dancing a jig. 'I'm in the team! I'm in the team!'

Simon, standing between the goal posts, with the ball, looked amazed.

'Wish I was,' said Jack.

'I'll tell them you're a great player, too,' Oscar promised. 'I'll tell them as soon as I've played against Silvertown. Hope I get a goal. Then they'll want me for *every* match.'

'Got your kit yet?' asked Simon, kicking the ball as high as he could.

'Not yet,' replied Oscar, waiting for the ball to fall.

Then he trapped it,

flicked it up

and hit it into the net.

'Very good,' said Jack. 'I can see why they picked you.'

'Got to go now,' Oscar announced after that success. 'Things to do at home.'

Simon wasn't sorry to see him go. He didn't like being beaten by someone's first shot at goal. Jack wasn't much good at shooting; he was better defending.

The moment he reached home, Oscar darted to his room for his mouth organ. Then, blowing a merry tune, he went to find his mum.

'Ah,' she said, 'a merry tune! You must have good news. Right, Oscar?'

'The best!' he told her, adding a final trill to his tune. 'I've been picked for Fotherby! Mum, please can I have their shirt? Oh, and some *real* boots? *Please.*'

She smiled, 'Must be your lucky day all round. I'm just off to the shops. If you'd come home five minutes later you'd have missed me. And I've just been paid a bonus for finishing some work ahead of time. So I'll treat you to the shirt; and the boots can be for your birthday next month. Grandad will be glad to get them for you. He was asking me what you needed.'

They went at once, very fast, because Oscar's mum always drove fast. Oscar knew the shops would have the right shirts: red-and-white stripes with the numbers in black.

'I'd like Number 3, please,' he told the shopkeeper.

'Oh, most boys want No. 9 or No. 7,' the man replied.

'I'm different,' Oscar pointed out.

'I can tell that,' remarked the young man, smiling at them. He invited Oscar to try on a shirt, but Oscar's mum said there wasn't time for that because she had other shopping to do. 'So let's see the boots,' she added, brisk as ever.

Oscar tried on four pairs before he found the perfect fit. 'If your boots don't feel right you can't kick properly,' he told his mum.

'You're dead right there,' said the salesman, winking at Oscar's mum.

'We'll go and see Grandad, show him the boots he's giving you,' she told him after finishing the shopping.

'You can let him see how you can kick.'

Grandad lived in a small house with a big garden, a grassy garden big enough to play football in. Oscar pulled on his boots the moment they arrived.

'They look good,' said Grandad, nodding and stroking his neat beard. 'Let's see if they score goals.'

He collected his football from the shed and placed two plant pots in front of the tall hedge. 'Right!' he said, tossing the ball high in the air, 'see what you can do with that, Oz.'

Oscar ran forward, waited for the ball to bounce and then hit it with all his might. It flew past the goalie's right shoulder at great speed and stuck in the hedge.

Grandad blinked. 'Well,' he said, 'those are real shooting boots. If you keep hitting shots like that you'll get a netful of goals, Oscar.'

Oscar jumped up and down with glee. Then, to show that his first goal wasn't a fluke, he scored another. By now it was almost dark and stars were winking. Grandad put his arm round Oscar and pointed to the sky above the little house.

'See that bright star twinkling up there?' he said. 'Well, that's your soccer star. Everyone's got a special star. Yours is that really bright one. Shows *you* are going to be a real soccer star, Grandson.'

Chapter Two

THAT NIGHT, OSCAR was too excited to sleep.
As soon as he dropped off, he woke up again.
So he gazed at his new football shirt, hanging
up by his toy cupboard. There wasn't much
light in the room, but the red-and-white stripes
showed up clearly. He gazed, too, at his boots,
standing beside the bed. Then he got up to
gaze at the stars. Which one had Grandad
pointed out? There were just so many –
millions, he supposed – that he couldn't be
sure he'd spotted the right one. But he knew

it was up there. One was brighter than the rest. That was his star, he felt sure.

He was so happy, he wanted to play his mouth organ. Surely one toot wouldn't awaken anyone? But first he was going to try on his shirt and boots again. Good boots, he'd been told, should fit like socks. In the dark, he pulled them on and then aimed a kick or two. What a pity his football was in the hall cupboard. Then, by mistake, he kicked the leg of his bedside table – and his water glass fell off. The noise was terrible.

Oscar was trying to pull the bedclothes over
his head when his mother burst into his room.
'What on earth are you up to?' she demanded.
Then she saw his feet. 'And who said you
could wear your new boots in bed, eh?'

'Boots?' he said, trying to sound amazed. His
mother wasn't fooled. She rarely was.

'Get them off at once,' she ordered. 'You'll be
playing no more football if you go on like this.
Now, off to sleep with you. And not another
sound. Understood?'

She left, taking the boots with her. She hadn't
said a word about the water glass, just
picked it up and put it back on
the table. Oscar was glad she
hadn't noticed he had his
new shirt on. At least he
could sleep in that – and
dream of winning the
match for Fotherby.
How many goals
would he
score?

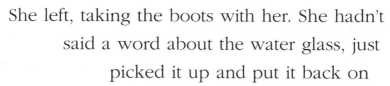

Chapter Three

NEXT MORNING HIS mum said, as she poured milk on his flakes: 'By the way, when is the big match?'

'Sunday, April 6th, at 11.30. The kick-off is early because . . .'

'What!' her hand flew to her mouth. 'But you can't play then! That's the big lunch day, your grandparents' special wedding anniversary party. Everyone's got to be there, you included.'

Oscar frowned. 'What's a wedding anniver-whatever-you-said?'

'Gran and Grandad have been married for

thirty years on that date, their wedding-birthday, you could call it. They want to celebrate that. We all do. Sorry, love, but you'll just have to play football another day.'

She was calm again and started to spoon up her flakes and slices of banana.

Oscar had stopped eating. His mouth felt as if it were full of glue. 'But this is an important match. My *first* big match. I *can't* miss it.'

His mum gave him a big smile and leaned across to pat his hand. 'Sorry, love, but a party like this comes first. Must do. Only happens once every thirty years. Think of that. They'll want you there, you *know* that. We can't let them down.'

'But Grandad says I'm going to be a star, a soccer star. He said so last night. I can't be a star if I don't play, can I?'

'True,' his mother admitted. 'But it's also true that you can't go and play on that day, Oscar. Sorry, but your grandparents come first. Now, don't go on about it! Don't start one of your tantrums. There'll be plenty of other soccer matches for you in the future.'

Oscar scowled. He'd been ready to blow up, or 'have a tantrum' as his mother always called it. But perhaps it wasn't worth it at the moment. His best plan would be to talk to Grandad and get him to say he could play on the anniv-whatever-it-was day.

'Can I take my boots to school, Mum? *Please.*'

He was sure she'd say no: but he was wrong.
'Well, just this once, to make up for your
disappointment over missing the match,' she
said, and even smiled.

It had worked!

'Can we go and see Grandad tonight?' Oscar
asked his mum as she drove him to school on
her way to her morning office job. 'Look,
you're not going to try and get round him so
you can miss the anniversary lunch,' she said
firmly. 'It's all fixed and it can't be changed
now. You've just got to accept that football
can't come first all the time.'

At school Oscar could hardly wait for playtime to arrive. When it did, he rushed to his bag to pull on his boots and then dashed into the playground.

'Hey, this isn't a real match, you know,' Jack pointed out, eyeing the spotless boots. 'It's just a bit of a kick around.'

'But I'm in training,' Oscar replied. 'I've got to get my boots feeling right for, for –' He couldn't say what he wanted to say. He now had no idea when he was going to play in a real match, wearing his new boots and his No. 3 shirt.

Luckily, the ball came his way and he kicked it, hit it hard and hit it low and hit it straight.

It went through a crowd of boys and girls and smacked against the stone wall, just inside the line chalked as a goal post. Nobody had ever scored a goal from that distance.

'Great shot!' yelled Tim, the captain of Fotherby, who was in the class above Oscar's. 'I knew I was right to pick you for the match.'

Oscar didn't know whether to be sad or

happy, but he knew his boots were wonderful. He'd never hit such a terrific shot in any other footwear. Perhaps they were truly magic boots. Perhaps . . .

'Tonight we're having some practice, as soon as we can all get there after tea,' Tim told his team. 'Behind Buzza's barn. Everybody's got to be there, or else.'

When Tim said 'or else' they all knew it meant if they failed to turn up they'd not be picked for the next match. Tim was a strong skipper. Usually he played part of the match in attack and part in defence. Within a couple of minutes after kick-off, he always seemed to know how good the other team was. He was brilliant.

Oscar took off his boots for the rest of the morning and thought about what he might do at lunchtime. But it started to rain, heavily, so no one was allowed out to play after lunch. The boots stayed in their bag while Oscar read a soccer story and watched streams of rain slide down the windows.

Chapter Four

'GRANDAD'S INVITED HIMSELF for tea but
I don't want you going on at him about that
match,' his mum said when he got home.

'But I've got to go out after tea, *got* to,'
Oscar told her, knowing what she would say.

She said it. 'Now, look, if this is about football
again, you'd better forget it. If Grandad's kind
enough to come and see us, the least we can
do is to stay in and welcome him. No arguing,
please, and no tantrums. And not a word to
Grandad about that match. That's an order,
Oscar.'

Oscar felt awful. Why was *everything* going wrong for him? He sometimes thought about running away from home, and he thought about it now. But he knew he wasn't old enough to be taken on as a full-time player by a big football club. And he couldn't think of anywhere else to run to. So he'd have to stay at home and get his own way. Somehow.

He wandered up to his room, trying to decide what to do. His shirt was still draped over the back of his chair. For a few moments he stood and looked at it, then walked round the chair, admiring the shirt from every angle. It was the best thing he'd worn in his whole life.

'Tea's ready and Grandad's coming up the path,' his mum called. 'Come down now.'

Oscar dithered for only a moment: he just *had* to put the shirt on. He couldn't last another hour without wearing it. So he pulled it on and went to admire himself in the mirror.

'Come down NOW, Oscar!' his mum thundered. 'This INSTANT. Or else . . .'

He went, still wearing the shirt, guessing what his mother would say when she saw it. Still, his fingers were crossed.

'My, that looks smart, really smart,' Grandad greeted him. 'I never had a football shirt as smart as that, Oz. Goes just right with those magic boots of yours.'

Oscar grinned and went to give his Grandad

a kiss. Amazingly, his mum didn't say a word against football all through the meal. Grandad kept on about the game so, of course, Oscar had to reply to be polite.

'So when are you going to wear those magic boots again?' Grandad asked as he tackled his second iced bun (Grandad could get away with anything at Mum's house). 'I am dying to see you score another of those brilliant goals.'

Oscar glanced at his mother. She raised her

eyebrows and closed her eyes but she didn't
say a word. She didn't say: 'Don't tell him about
the practice game.' So Oscar said: 'Well, our
skipper wants us to train tonight at Buzza's Barn.
Everybody's got to be there. After tea, he said.'

'Champion! Can I come, too?' Grandad asked.

Oscar looked at his mum, who just shook her
head this time. But he didn't think that meant
he couldn't go out. He guessed she'd given up
trying to tell him what he must do. That
sometimes happened when Grandad was
present. Grandad was good at getting his own
way, Oscar realised.

'That'd be great, Grandad,' he said eagerly,

and even refused the chance of another bun so they could hurry away. Grandad was a fast eater and he'd already had his share of everything on the table.

'Is he a football manager?' Tim asked when they reached the grassy area behind the big barn where Farmer Buzza kept his tractors and hay and a shiny silver car that took part in big parades. Tim was looking at Grandad, who was wearing his best black hat and a football scarf.

'No, he's my Grandad,' Oscar explained. 'He's just come to see me play in my new boots.'

'That's a pity,' said Tim, addressing Grandad. 'I hoped you were looking for new players for your team.'

'Ah, but I keep my eyes open and tell the right people when I see something good, when I see a future star player,' Grandad replied. 'So play your best, you boys.'

They did. But Oscar didn't manage to score a goal, which made Grandad sad. Still, they weren't really practising shooting. Tim had seen a training film on TV so they were all practising free kicks and long passes and heading. Tim said Silvertown would be hard to beat, so Fotherby had to be in top form. It was almost dark when Tim decided they'd done enough training for one night.

'Thank you for watching us,' Tim said politely to Grandad. 'I didn't expect you to stay so long. I hope you enjoyed it.'

'Oh, I did, young Tim,' Grandad replied, beaming. 'I think you have the makings of a top team. So I hope you have a really good win against – who is it? – oh yes, Silvertown. You *must* beat them.'

On their way home Oscar wondered what to say about that game. Should he plead with

Grandad to be excused from the anniv-whatever-it-was lunch? But what would Mum say if Grandad told her what he'd done? Before he could make up his mind, however, Grandad turned aside and stepped into the Big Corner Store, a shop where he bought his favourite mint balls and some sweets for Oscar (the sort of sweets Mum never bought).

'This place seems to expand like a balloon,' Grandad remarked, looking at new shelves packed with videos.

'Ah, that is why it is called The Big Store,' smiled Mr Dev, the owner. 'Soon I will call it

The Biggest Store!'

'Sometimes we get our videos here,' Oscar said. 'Tim does, too. His dad is camera mad so sometimes he makes his own videos. Tim likes the football ones best. He'd watch *anything* to do with soccer.'

'Look, we must choose our sweets now,' Grandad pointed out, 'because I've got to get off home. A young chap like me needs his sleep, you know.'

Mr Dev smiled again and added a couple of extra sweets to the bag when Oscar had made his choice. Grandad sucked noisily on a mint ball as they strolled towards Oscar's house.

'Grandad, can I be excused from the anniv-whatever-it-is lunch?' Oscar burst out when they

reached the gate. 'I mean, I'd love to be there – but I'd love to play in the football match even more.'

Grandad laughed. 'I like your honesty, Oscar! Well, I'll have to think about it. Your mum wants *everybody* to be at that lunch, you know. No excuses allowed for not being there. But, well, I have an idea how we could manage something. You see, I'd love to watch you in that match against Silvertown, and I expect your mum would, too. I want to see you become a soccer star. I want that very much. But I can't leave Grandma on that day of all days, can I? Wouldn't be right. So you'll have to keep your fingers crossed my idea works out.'

Then, as they were about to enter the house, Grandad held Oscar's arm, whispering: 'Don't say a word about my idea to your mum. Trust me.'

'I trust you, Grandad,' Oscar replied. But he couldn't say anything to his mum because he hadn't a clue what Grandad's idea was!

Chapter Five

ON SUNDAY MORNING, April 6th, Oscar was so excited he could hardly eat his breakfast.

'Come on, that's not like you,' his mum urged. 'You won't be here for lunch, so eat your breakfast. Food is energy, you know. You'll need all your strength.'

Oscar nodded. He knew he needed lots of energy to play better than anybody else in his first match for Fotherby. The star of the match, that's what he was going to be. Grandad said he was looking forward to hearing about every kick and had promised to save him a huge piece of the lemon pie they were having at the anniv-er-sary lunch. Oscar was looking forward to sitting next to Grandad and eating it while he recalled the game. It was the least he could do after his grandparents had excused him from being at the special lunch.

So, he ate as much as he could because he didn't want his mum to change her mind. Somehow Grandad had convinced her that for once football ought to come first for Oscar.

After breakfast his parents went upstairs to get ready for the lunch party, so Oscar put on his boots and had some shooting practice in the garden. He put up stakes in place of goalposts and then pushed the dustbin into the space between them to act as a goalie. Bang! His first shot was

so hard it knocked the dustbin over, scattering
rubbish everywhere, so he had to scramble
around, collecting it all. But that made him take
better aim next time. He managed
a couple of goals and hit the
dustbin only twice.
So he thought
he was
in good
form.

Then his mum yelled from the window that Tim's father had arrived to pick him up.

'Have a good time, and don't forget to score that goal for Grandad,' she said as she waved them off. 'You promised!'

'Hey, what's this about scoring goals?' Tim asked. 'You're playing in defence, not attack. I told you that on Friday.'

'I know, Tim,' Oscar agreed. 'But, well, my Grandad can't come to the match so I said I'd get a goal for him, if I could. I mean, well, I might, mightn't I?'

'Shouldn't think so,' Tim said with a shake of his head. 'I want you to stay back, not charge up front, trying to be a hero. You've got to play for the team, not  for yourself. I need your strong kicking from the back. Anyway, No. 3 is always a defender.'

'Still, you never know, Oscar might hit the winner from the halfway line,' Tim's father remarked when they got out of the car. He collected his video camera from the boot. 'So, shoot if you get the chance, Oscar, and keep your fingers crossed you hit the back of the net. *Their* net, that is!'

Oscar felt a bit upset, but not bad enough to make him play badly. He knew it was important to think about the team. Fotherby needed to win this match, to go on to win the Cup. He wanted to score goals, but he would defend as if his life depended on it.

Silvertown were strong and fast and eager. So Oscar and his team-mates had a lot of defending to do right from the start. Even Tim, who liked to go forward, had to stay back to help out. Twice Fotherby players made desperate clearances on their own goal-line. So, somehow, the score remained 0-0. Tim's father hadn't used up much film yet. He was waiting to capture Fotherby's goals.

Near the end of normal time, with everyone thinking there'd have to be a replay, Oscar

made a good tackle just outside his own penalty area. With the ball at his feet now, he decided to run. Silvertown defenders just backed off, expecting him to pass the ball. But he didn't, he kept running, fast and straight. He went right into their penalty area and was lining up to shoot when a defender brought him crashing down.

A penalty kick! It had to be. As Tim ran up, Oscar got to his feet, unhurt.

'*Please* let me take the kick, Tim,' Oscar pleaded. 'Go on. You know I've got the hardest kick.'

Tim glanced at his father, now moving behind the goal, his camera ready to film. Tim's dad nodded. 'Oscar earned the penalty,' he said.

'Okay,' said Tim. 'But don't miss.'

'I won't,' Oscar promised. And he didn't. He hit the ball so hard that the goalie didn't even see it go past him into the roof of the net. Oscar leapt into the air with joy and his team-mates almost smothered him. He wished he had his mouth organ with him to give a toot.

It was the winning goal because there wasn't time for more goals to be scored. Fotherby were through to the next round of the Cup – and Oscar had scored a goal for Grandad. If *only* Grandad could have seen it, he thought.

Tim's father came up to him. 'Here you are, Oscar,' he said. 'This is for your grandad – and all your family. It's the video he asked me to make for him so he could have his anniversary lunch and see the match. He said he'd show it to everyone tonight.'

Oscar was amazed. So that was how his grandad had got round his mum to let him off the lunch! Trust Grandad! He grinned.

'You'll be the star of the film, scoring a goal like that,' Tim remarked.

A soccer star, just as Grandad had described him. But Oscar wasn't going to tell his team-mates that. It would sound like boasting.

'Tim, can I play as a forward next time?' he asked the Fotherby skipper.

'Just as long as you score a goal every game,' Tim replied.

'I will,' Oscar promised. And he hurried home to the anniv-football filmshow.

Yellow Bananas are bright, funny, brilliantly imaginative stories written by some of today's top writers. All the books are beautifully illustrated in full colour.

So if you've enjoyed this story, why not pick another from the bunch?

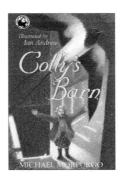